Mafia's Nanny

Juliet Verber

Contents

Chapter 1

"You need to find a job" my best friend told me while we were walking through the mall. "I can't find a good job that pays enough! Why don't you help me for once" I raise my voice at her.

She's been annoying me about getting a job for a month but refuses to help me get one. "You said you liked kids right?" She asks me. "Yeah I do why?" I ask.

"Because my boss is looking for a nanny to take care of his 6 year old daughter. You get paid pretty good and get to live there. Interviews are tomorrow. I can stay the night with you and we can go to his place together" she tells me. I know she works in the mafia already so nothing that happens would surprise me.

"Wait so I'll get a job and be living with you?" I ask her excitedly.
"Yup" she says calmly somehow. "Let's go to my place now then" I
say and we leave the mall.

When they get to Athena's apartment

"I forgot how small and dirty your apartment was" Aphrodite says
and I give her a dirty look. She wasn't wrong though. It was just a
small, dirty apartment. It's also falling apart.

"Shut up lets just go to bed" I tell her and we both go to my
room. I pick out and outfit for the interview and get into bed with
Aphrodite.

In the morning

"Bitch hurry up and get changed!" Aphrodite yells at me. "I'm coming let me just put my shoes on!" I yell back.

(Athena's outfit)

(Athena's shoes)

"All my stuff is in your car right?" I ask Aphrodite. We decided the
best idea was to pack my stuff in case I get the job. If I don't we can
just bring it back.

"Yup now let's go before we are late!" She yells back. We leave the apartment and get into her car.

When they get to Dante's

Aphrodite just opens the door since she lives there. I follow her to where all the other girls are waiting. "Wait here for your name to be called" she tells me and then walks away.

I looked at all the other girls and notice they are all wearing revealing clothing. Some of them give me dirty looks as I sit down. After 30 minutes my name is called so I go to the office.

"You must be Athena. I hear your Aphrodite's friend" the guy sitting at the desk says when I walk in. "Yeah. I've known Aphrodite since I was 17" I tell him and sit down.

"I'm not gonna lie to you, your the only one that actually dressed properly" he tells me smiling. I laugh at his comment. "So I know everything I need to know about you and your experience. The only thing we need to do is introduce you to my daughter to see if she likes you" he tells me.

After he says that Aphrodite walks in with a little girl in her arms. "Dante! Your child won't let go of me!" She whines. I stand up and walk over to her. Aphrodite immediately hands Luna to me and Luna looks at me like she's investigating me.

"Your really pretty" she tells me after investigating my face. "Aww thank you, what's your name princess?" I ask her. "My name is Luna!" She says "Daddy! She called me a princess!" Dante laughs at her. "I know she did. Luna this is Athena. She's gonna be your new nanny" he tells her.

"Really?! Can we go color Athena!?" She asks me loudly and I look at Dante for permission. "Aphrodite says she has your stuff so I will get someone to put it in your room and someone will show you to your room later" he tells me giving me permission to go play with Luna.

I nod and walk out of his office. I put Luna down and let her lead me to her room.

Later when Luna is in bed

I go back to Dante's office now that Luna is in bed. I just walk in without knocking and he looks up immediately. "Oh it's just you. Did you need something? Is something wrong?" He asks worried.

"Nothings wrong I just need to know where my room is" I tell him and he gets up. "Follow me" he says walking out of his office and down the hall. He stops in front of a door.

"This is your room" he says and points to the door down the hall. "That's my room. Please don't go in without permission" he says and walks back to his office.

I go into my room to see all my stuff is already out away. I get changed into comfy clothes and get into my bed. I decided to go to bed early since it was a long day.

Chapter 2

"Athenaaaaa! Can we go in the pool?!" Luna yelled running into my room. "Of course princess. Let's go get your swimsuit on" I say and we walk to her room. "What one do you want to wear princess? The pink or the purple?" I ask her and show them to her. "The purple of course!" I laugh at her words.

(Luna's swimsuit)

"I should have known. Now do you want help getting changed?" I asked her.

"No I can do it myself" she says giggling. "Ok well I'm gonna go get my swimsuit on. Yell to me if you need me and don't go to the pool without me" I tell her while walking out of her room. Once I get to my room I pick out a swimsuit and put it on.

(Athena's swimsuit)

I go back to her room and see that she's not there. I start freaking out and run to Dante's office, I run in forgetting to knock. "This better be important if you couldn't take the time to fucking knock!" Dante yells at me without looking up.

I notice that Luna is on his lap and calm down. "I'm so sorry, Sir. I didn't know where Luna went and I started freaking out. I just forgot to knock-" Luna then cuts me off "Athena! Tell daddy to go swimming with us please" I look at him with a confused look.

"I'm sorry for yelling, I wouldn't have yelled if I knew it was you. She's been in here begging me to go swimming with you guys and she won't take no for an answer" he says sounding a bit annoyed.

"I'm sorry for leaving her unattended I was getting changed. Luna come on let's go swimming now" I say walking up to her and Dante. "No I want daddy to go swimming with us!" She whines.

I look at Dante not knowing what to say. "Fine, go down to the pool with Athena while I get get changed" he says looking at Luna. I giggle a bit when Luna jumps off Dante's lap and runs out of his office.

"I'll be down in a couple minutes" he said to me while we walked out of his office. We went our separate ways and I grabbed my knife and 2 towels then headed to the pool.

I see Luna is already there and quickly put my towel on a chair, hiding my knife under my towel and putting her towel on the chair beside mine.

"Come on! Get in Athena!" Luna yells while laughing. "I'm coming princess" I say while walking into the pool. Dante shows up 5 minutes later.

"Daddy!!" Luna yells. I turn around seeing that Dante is getting in the pool. "Took him long enough didn't it princess" I say laughing. Dante actually smiles at my comment.

"Look Athena! You made daddy smi-" Dante cuts her off by splashing her. After 10 minutes of playing in the pool Anastasia comes to the pool. "Luna! Get out of the pool, go upstairs, and pick up your toys! NOW!" She yells at Luna. Luna looks at me scared. "Luna... why don't you get your princess towel and go wait for me in my room? I have a gift for you."

Luna looks at me excited and gets out. She gets her towel and runs to my room. I laugh at her excitement a little and then look at Anastasia. "What the actual fuck is your problem?!" I yell at her. "She didn't pick up her toys" she said shrugging.

"That's not your business! It doesn't even effect you! I'm the one that's taking care of her so I'm that one that tells her what to do! You do not have the right to come ruin our fun and yell at her! Where are these toys that she didn't pick up?!" I yell at her, annoyed by her smugness.

"In her room, but that doesn't matter!" She says looking at me like I'm insane. "It does matter! They are in her room where they are supposed to be!" I think she's stupid at this point

"You don't know anything about kids! You dress like a child yourself, you don't know how to take care of a child!" She yells at me while laughing. Suddenly I see Aphrodite and Antonio run over to see what the yelling is about.

"Excuse me?! The way I dress does not have anything to do with how well I can take care of children! And you can't judge the way I dress when you dress like that!" I yell and she looks at me insulted.

"What do you mean! I dress nicely!" She says while looking me up and down with a disgusted look on her face. "Yeah, if nicely means slutty. Slutty is ok sometimes like when your going to a club but on the daily?! Yeah fuck no. Your literally a whore"

"Dante! Are you not gonna say something to her!" She looks at him but he just ignores her. "I'm the whore?! You were literally a stripper before! You shouldn't even be allowed around children!" She yells at me and smiles thinking she won.

"How do you know about that?! HOW THE FUCK DO YOU KNOW ABOUT THAT YOU BITCH!" I scream at her while getting out of the pool. "NO ONE KNOWS ABOUT THAT EXCEPT MY BEST FRIEND!" I screamed while Dante held me back so I couldn't get out of the pool.

"Let me go Dante! LET ME GO!" I yell kicking him. "Dante let her go!" Aphrodite yells and Dante lets me go. I immediately get out of the pool when he lets me go. "You stupid fucking whore" I mumbled while getting the knife from under my towel.

I walk up to her with the knife and put it in her face. "DO YOU HAVE A FUCKING DEATH WISH?!" I scream at her. Dante immediately gets out of the pool and comes up behind me. "Anastasia... you had no right to say anything you did. Get the fuck out of my house right now!" He says to her but she doesn't move.

"I SAID NOW ANASTASIA!" He yells getting impatient. I flinched at his voice behind me. Anastasia finally leaves but nobody else moves. "Antonio, Aphrodite, leave us" Dante finally says after a minute of silence.

Once they are gone he grabs my knife from me and gets his towel. "Go change and meet me in my office" he says calmly and leaves to go change.

I stand there for a minute thinking about what just happened. I finally grab my towel and go to my room. I see Luna sitting on my bed crying and immediately run up to her. "Luna what's wrong? Why are you crying princess?" I ask her worried.

"Am I in trouble?" She whispers while crying. "No of course your not in trouble. Why would you be in trouble?" I ask her while getting changed. "Because I didn't pick up my toys" she says.

(Athena's dress and shoes)

"Luna. I never told you to pick up your toys. You don't have to listen to Anastasia. You listen to me." I tell her grabbing the gift I got her. "Here" I say putting the crown on her head. "Now you are a real princess! And I have one to!" I say smiling.

(Athena's crown)

(Luna's crown)

She looks up at me smiling. "Your the best Athena!" She then jumps up and hugs me. "Thank you Luna. Do you wanna show your dad our crowns?" I ask her laughing a bit. "YES!" She yells and runs out of my room.

I follow her into Dante's office and see her on Dantes lap again. I smile at the sight until Luna yells "Look daddy! Athena also has a crown!" Dante immediately looks at me when she says that.

"Luna. Go to your room while me and Athena talk" he says with no emotion on his face. She walks out but stops at the door and says "don't be mad at her daddy. I like her and I don't want her to leave" then she goes to her room.

"Athena, please sit" he sighs. I sit down and look at my lap, to scared to look at him. "Would you care to explain what Anastasia said about you being a stripper?" He says after noticing I wasn't going to start the conversation.

"I tried to cover it up. I'm really poor and I couldn't find a stable job that could support my needs when my parents abandoned me. I was just trying to be a bartender but the owner of the club made me sign a contract. I didn't read it before signing it and it turned out to be a contract forcing me to be a stripper for a year" I said trying not to cry.

"Ok... why didn't you tell me?" He says slowly trying not to make me cry. "Because I have trauma from working there... the only person who knows anything about this is Aphrodite" I tell him hoping he won't ask me anymore questions.

"That's it for now. I'll talk to you again later" he said fast. I looked at him confused for a second, then got up and walked out of his office. I go to Luna's room to find her picking up her toys.

"Princess, what are you doing? I said you didn't have to pick up your toys" I said confused. She looked at me and I saw tears rolling down her face. I run up to her and pick her up.

"Princess, what happened? Why are you crying?" I asked trying to stay calm. "Miss Anastasia came in and told me I had to clean up my toys and when I told her you said I didn't have to she said she would tell my daddy and get me in a lot of trouble" she whispered through her crying.

"She said daddy would take all my toys away Athena" she tells me sniffling. "Luna, stay in here until I come back" I tell her while putting in on her bed. She nods and I walk out and go to the kitchen to find Anastasia.

_____Thanks for reading!

Chapter 3

"Hey slut!" I yell when I see her in the kitchen. She turns to look at me immediately and smirks "what do you want kid" she says laughing. "You are so fucking lucky Dante took my knife. Cause I wouldn't hesitate to fucking stab you right now!" I told her knowing if I grabbed a kitchen knife he would fire me for using it to stab her.

"Dante your whore of a nanny is trying to hurt me!" She screams and Dante comes running into the kitchen. "What the fuck are you screaming about Anastasia?!" He raises his voice at her immediately.

"Your stupid nanny was threatening me for no reason" she said fake crying. He looked at me confused. "She told Luna to clean her room and if she didn't she would tell you and you would get mad. She also said you would take all her toys away" I said glaring at Anastasia.

Dante looked at me with a surprised face but it disappeared in a matter of seconds. "Didn't I tell you to get out of my fucking house Anastasia" he says looking back at her angry.

"Come on baby. You know you were just angry. You don't actually want me to leave" she says seductively. I giggle at her stupidity but stop when she glares at me.

"Don't call me baby. We aren't together and we never will be. Get the fuck out of my house and don't come back!" He says obviously sick of her shit.

She runs out of the house and Dante turns to me. "I'm going to my office" he says and walks away.

Skip to when Luna is in bed

I'm just sitting on my bed reading when Aphrodite runs in. "Get up bitch! We are going to the club!" She yells forcing me to get out of my bed.

She drags me to her room and pushes me on her bed. "Your wearing one of my dresses because all of yours are boring" she says going into her closet. "Please don't pick something super revealing" I whine.

She comes out with 2 black outfits and throws one at me. "Go into my bathroom and put it on" she tells me. I go into her bathroom and change.

(Athena's outfit)

I walk out of the bathroom and stare at Aphrodite.

(Aphrodite's outfit)

"Girl! You look so hot!" She yells looking me up and down. "Bitch look at you! Everyone is gonna be looking at you!" I yell back at her. I remember I'm supposed to tell Dante when I'm going somewhere.

"I have to tell Dante I'm going out with you" I tell her walking out of her room. She then grabs me and pulls me back into her room. "You forgot shoes bitch" she says handing me shoes.

(Aphrodite's shoes)

(Athena's shoes)

I put them on and run to Dante's office. I knock on the door this time. "Come in!" He yells so I can hear him and I go in. "What the fuck do you want" he says without look up.

"I'm sorry I was just gonna tell you I'm going out with Aphrodite..." I say quietly. He looks up immediately when he hears my voice. "Where are you going..." he says slowly while looking me up and down smirking.

"To a club.." I say looking at him confused. "Who else is going with you guys?" He says still looking at my body. "Just me and Aphrodite I think" I tell him. "Are you gonna look at me when talking to me" I say out of nowhere.

He stops inspecting my body and looks at my face. "You guys aren't going alone. I'll go with you" he says sternly. "Well we are leaving in a couple minutes so hurry up!" I yell while walking out of his office and going back to Aphrodite's room.

"Dante's going with us" I tell her hoping she won't get mad at me. "Of course he is. He would never let us go alone" she says annoyed, rolling her eyes.

5 minutes later. The girls are waiting for Dante downstairs.

We hear someone walking up to us and turn around to see who it is. We immediately see Dante walking up to us really fast.

(Dante's outfit)

I freeze, staring at him. "We gonna go or are you just gonna keep staring at me" he says suddenly while smirking. I look up at him and nod. Me and Aphrodite hold hands while following Dante to the car we are taking. We all get in the back and Dante tells the driver where we are going.

When they get there (pretend they have their ID's)

Me and Aphrodite get out of the car, still holding hands. "ID" the guy at the door says immediately. Me and Aphrodite hand him our ID's and wait for a minute. He finally gives them back and lets us in.

We go in leaving Dante to do his own thing. We immediately go up to the bar and sit down. "What can I get you beautiful girls tonight" a random bartender asks. "Whiskey" I say with a straight face.

He looks at me surprised. "Are you sure you can handle whiskey?" He asks. Before I can say anything I hear Dante behind me. "Get her what she asked for. And I'll be paying" he says to the bartender.

I look back at Dante for a second then look back at the bartender to see a scared looked on his faces. "Yes sir" he says and immediately goes to get my drink.

I turn to Dante and look at him annoyed. "I could have dealt with it myself. I don't need you to baby me" I say really angry. He just looks at me and walks away to go sit at a booth in the corner.

I roll my eyes and turn back around to find the bartender standing in front of me with my drink. I take it from him and down it. "Get me another one" I say and look at Aphrodite.

Time skip. Athena is drunk

I look over to see Dante staring at me and Aphrodite dancing. Suddenly I feel someone behind me. They grab my waist and start grinding on me. "Hey! Get off me!" I yell while trying to push him away.

"Get the fuck away from her" I look up to see Dante standing in front of me. The random guy lets go and Dante opens his arms. I immediately walk into his arms and hug him.

"Sorry man. I didn't know she was yours" the random guy says walking away. I look around for Aphrodite and see her dancing with a guy.

Dante takes me over to where he was sitting and I notice all the guys that were sitting with him are staring at me with wide eyes.

I giggle a bit and Dante pulls me on his lap. "Who's she?" One of the guys sitting at the table asks. I look at him and analyze his face. "None of your business bitch" I say to him smiling.

"Excuse me?! Who the fuck do you think you are!?" He says angry. "You look like an angry chihuahua" I say laughing at him. "Dante control your bitch!" Another one of the guys say.

"I'm not his bitch! I'm Aphrodite's bitch" I say still smiling. Suddenly I see a shadow beside me. I look over to see that it's Aphrodite. "Oh hi slut" I greet Aphrodite.

"Hello bitch" she says back laughing. "Aphrodite can you control your bitch?! She's insulting us!" The angry chihuahua says. I hear Dante laugh and look at him. "What the fuck are you laughing at" I say without thinking.

"James, shut your mouth. Athena is perfectly fine" Aphrodite says to the angry chihuahua. "And she's not my bitch. She's my best friend" she laughs at James.

"Oh that's his name?! I was just calling him angry chihuahua" I tell Aphrodite and she laughs really hard. I smile at my success. "Well if she's not your bitch then she's Dante's bitch. So Dante fucking control your bitch before I kill her!" James yells getting angrier then before.

"Your not gonna fucking touch her. If you do I will kill you and your fucking family" Dante says looking at him. If looks could kill, James would have died on the spot.

I look at Dante's face and start analyzing it. "What are you doing Athena?" He asks while putting his empty glass down. "Analyzing your face" I say keeping a straight face.

"Why are you analyzing my face?" He asks looking at me confused. "Because I'm trying to figure out if I like it or not" I tell him while grabbing the sides of his face and turning it.

"Athena. Be gentle. And are you telling me my face is ugly" he says and all the guys at the table laugh, except James of course. "I am being gentle! And I never said your face is ugly dumbass" I turn his face the other way.

"You are really close to my face Athena" he says in a warning tone. I ignore his comment and keep analyzing his face. "She's really close to kissing him" one of the guys say.

"She's to much of a coward to kiss him" James says. I freeze when I hear him say that and Dante looks at me, trying to figure out what I'm thinking. "Athena... is something wrong?" Dante asks, worried.

"Everything's fine" I say and go back to analyzing Dante's face. "How much you wanna bet, James" the guy said. "10k that she won't kiss him, deal Mark?" James says lowering his voice, but I still hear him.

"Deal" Mark said. I stop analyzing Dante's face and think about what I want to do. I grab Dante's drink from his hand and down it. "What the fuck are you drinking" I say disgusted.

"Beer" he said laughing at my expression. "That was not beer! That was piss or something!" I say loudly and everyone sitting at the table laughs. Including James.

I give him his glass back and turn my body so I can put my head in his neck. "Can I do something. Mark and James made a bet and I don't want James to win" I whisper so only Dante can hear me and I lift my head.

"What is it?" He whispers. "James said I was to much of a coward to kiss you and I don't want him to get 10k" I whisper back. He thinks about it for a minute. "Sure" he whispers and laughs a little.

"I want another whiskey" I say in a normal voice and Aphrodite gets me one. I down it immediately when she gives it to me and some of the guys gasp. "You are gonna be so hungover in the morning and I'm gonna have to take care of you and Luna" Dante says a bit annoyed.

I smile and kiss him for at least 5 seconds then pull away. "You will be fine. I'm not that hard to deal with. Just keep that stupid whore, Anastasia, away from me and everything will be fine" I say looking over at the guys. I see James giving Mark a stack of cash and start laughing making them look up at me.

I turn my head back around and hide it in Dante's neck. "Fucking idiot" I mumble making Dante laugh quietly. "I think we are gonna get going now" he says standing up. "I'm not walking you have to carry me" I tell him while putting my arms around his neck.

"Come on Athena! Let's go dance!" Aphrodite yells while dragging off Dante's lap. I'm just dancing with Aphrodite when I feel hands on my waist.

Sorry for the random change in the story. I had a last minute idea that I wanted to add. Also left y'all on a cliffhanger with this one. Love you guys!

Chapter 4

I turn to see Dante. I immediately know he's drunk. "Dante... what's wrong?" I hesitate. I don't want him to get mad at me. "Nothing. You just look so beautiful" he mumbles, hiding his face in my neck.

"Come on Dante, let's go sit down" I take one of his hands off my waist and hold it, pulling him back to the table. I make him sit down and then sit on his lap, facing the table. "Your so pretty" I hear Dante mumble.

"How much did he drink?" I ask the guys. "Like 5 Beers since you went to dance with Aphrodite" James tells me. "Seriously?! Why?!" I said sounding really annoyed. "Because he was sad you walked away" Mark speaks up.

"You could have came and danced with us" I tell Dante in a soft voice.

"I don't know how to dance" he mumbles. "I could have taught you" I laugh a bit. "Can I have a kiss?" He mumbles into my neck so only I can hear him.

"Not tonight" I tell him, blushing. "Whyyyy" he whines. "Because your gonna regret it tomorrow" I want to kiss him though.

When we got home I helped Dante get to his room and tucked him. Once he's tucked in I go to my room and immediately pass out when I lay down.

In the morning

"Athena!! Athena wake up!" Luna runs into my room waking me up. "Whyyy" I whine. "Because I wanna go shopping today!!" She yelled jumping on me.

"Ok ok! I'm up!" I laugh getting out of my bed. "Let me get changed first" I saying going into my closet. "Can I pick your outfit?! Pleaseeee?!" Luna begs, following me into my closet.

"Of course princess" I smile.

(Athena's outfit)

"I love it Luna! Now what about shoes?" I say after I change into the dress. "These ones go with the dress!" she says handing me heels.

(Athena's heels)

"Alright! Now let's go get your outfit" I say walking to her room. She follows me in. "Can you pick out my outfit!" She asks and I go into her closet.

"Of course I can!" I say picking out a dress. "Put this dress on while I pick out shoes" I tell her giving her a dress.

(Luna's dress)

"And here's the shoes" I say giving her the shoes I picked.

(Luna's shoes)

"Luna, is your dad awake?" I ask her. "Yup! Follow me!!!" She says running out of her room, going to Dante's office. I follow behind her slowly so I don't fall.

"Dante" I say walking into his office. "Is it ok if I take Luna to the mall?" I ask. "Sure but I'm going with you. I don't want you guys going alone" he tells me getting up.

He looks me up and down and laughs a bit. "Why are you wearing a dress like that?" I look at him with a worried look. "Hey! I picked out her outfit!" Luna yells at him.

He looks at her with guilt in his eyes. "I'm sorry Luna. I didn't know you picked it out. It looks really good" he tells her, picking her up. "Are you really gonna go to the mall wearing that?" I ask him.

"Yes? What's wrong with my outfit?" He asks looking sad.

(Dante's outfit)

"I didn't say anything was wrong with it... It's just... no one goes to the mall in a suit.." I tell him hoping he doesn't get mad.

"Who cares what other people do! Now are we going to the mall or not?!" He says irritated. "Yeah let's go!" I say walking out of his office.

"Wait! Can I drive?!" I ask when we get to the garage. "No" he says getting into a car. I pout and help Luna get in the back. Once she's buckled I get into the passenger seat.

_____

This is a short chapter I'm so sorry! I just wanted to get a chapter out as soon as possible.

I hope it's good and I will try to get out more chapters as soon as possible.

I love you all so much and thank you for being so patient!

Chapter 5

When we get to the mall I get out and help Luna out of the car. "What store should we go to first?" I ask her while we walk inside the mall. "The toy store!" She yells, excited.

I laugh and we walk to the toy store, Dante following behind us. "Is there anywhere you want to go after the toy store?" He asks me. "I might go look at art supplies" I tell him as we walk into the toy store.

We follow Luna around the toy store for 10 minutes. "Alright Luna let's go pay now" I tell her and we start walking to cash. While the cashier scans the toys she picked out I grab my card from my purse.

Suddenly, a hand grabs my wrist. "Your not paying" I hear Dante say. "Why not?" I ask, turning to look at him. "Because she's my daughter" he says and pays.

As we walk out of the store I look over to Dante. I laugh at the sight of him. He's holding the 2 bags of toys that Luna got. When we get to the craft store I bend down to talk to Luna. "Would you like to go in with me?" I ask, assuming Dante wasn't going in.

"Yes!" She says jumping. I laugh and walk in. I grab a basket and take out my phone to look at my list. "Ok Luna, we need to get a paint palette, some paint brushes, some canvases, some paints, a sketch book, and pencils" I tell her.

"Why do you need so much stuff?" I jump at the sound of Dante's voice. "You scared me! I didn't know you came in with us!" I raise my voice at him without noticing.

"Not my fault" he says sounding angry. I ignore the tone in his voice and walk over to the paint palettes. "Luna would you like to pick one for me?" I ask her. "Yes please!" She says looking at all the palettes.

(The palette she chose)

"This one!" She says handing me a palette. I put it in my basket and we walk to the paint brushes. "I'm gonna pick the paint brushes cause I need specific ones" I tell Luna.

(The paint brushes)

I find the paint brushes and put them in my basket, then we walk to the sketch books. "You can pick a sketch book for me Luna" I tell her and she immediately starts looks at all them.

(The sketchbook)

She puts a sketchbook in my basket and we walk over to the pencils. I pick the pencils because I need specific ones again.

(The pencils) -Author note- I have these pencils

I put the pencils in my basket and we go to the paints.

(The acrylic paints she got)

I grab some acrylic paints and put them in my basket. I then walk over to the water color paints.

(The watercolor paints she got)

I grab water color paints and put them in my basket. "Last thing we need is canvases" I say and we walk over to the canvases. I get a couple canvases.

(The canvases)

"Ok I'm done. Let's go checkout" I tell Luna and Dante. We get to cash and the cashier scans all my items. I grab my card to pay but when I look up Dante is already paying with his card.

I decide to just talk to him when we get back to the house. Dante ends up taking all 3 of my bags. Me and Luna decide we are done shopping and want to go home so we all go get back in the car.

When they get home Luna eats and goes to bed

I put all my stuff away and change into pyjamas.

(Her pyjamas)

Once I'm changed I go to Dante's office. I don't knock and just walk in. "Your supposed to fucking knock!" He yells looking up, seeing me flinch.

I see guilt in his eyes for a second before it disappears. "Sorry. What did you need?" He asks and I go lay on the couch in his office. "I was wondering why you payed for my stuff today" I said, looking at the ceiling. "Because I wanted to" he says getting up grabbing a bottle.

He walks over to me with the bottle, picks up my legs, sits down on the couch, and puts my legs on his lap. I notice that the bottle is whiskey. He opens it, chugs a quarter of it, and hands it to me.

"What are you doing" I ask taking the bottle. "Drinking. Do you want some or not?" He asks and I chug the rest of the bottle. "Got anymore?" I ask.

1 hour later

Suddenly someone barges into the room. I look to see who it is and see it's Antonio. "What is happening in here... and why are there 5 empty bottles of whiskey on the floor?" He says with a confused expression on his face.

_____Another chapter for y'all even though it's pretty short!

I'm trying to write more for everyone who's been reading this. I just haven't had a lot of time lately so I appreciate the patience.

Hope everyone likes this chapter.

Chapter 6

Antonio looks between me and Dante. My head is on Dante's lap and Dante is shirtless. Wait when did that happen?

"We are drinking DuH" I say with an annoyed tone. I look at Dante to see he's already looking at me. "What are you looking at man whore?!" I yell at him.

"Aphrodite! Get in here please!" Antonio yells while laughing. Aphrodite immediately walks into Dante's office and stares at me. "Why is everyone staring at me! I know I'm pretty!" I yell and everyone laughs.

"Shut up! Stop laughing at me or I'll shoot you!" I say annoyed. Everyone stops laughing except Dante. I look at him, giving him the death stare. He doesn't stop laughing.

I immediately slap him across the face making Antonio and Aphrodite gasp. Dante looks at me angry. "What are you gonna do bitch boy?!" I yell getting up.

He gets up and towers over me. "I ain't scared of you! You won't do shit!" I yell looking up at him. "Aphrodite, Antonio, get out!" Dante yells and they both run out, shutting the door behind them.

I get a bit worried. He wouldn't hit me... right? He stares at me for a minute before pushing me to the ground. "You fucking whore!" He yells at me and I crawl away from him.

"I-I'm sorry Dante I wasn't thinking..." I mumble covering my head in the corner. Suddenly the door opens and Aphrodite runs over to me. She hands me headphones and my phone. I put them on without questioning her and play music.

Aphrodite stands beside Antonio while he yells at Dante. I take off the headphones not knowing he was yelling. "DANTE WHAT THE ACTUAL FUCK IS YOUR PROBLEM?!" Antonio yells.

I start having a hard time breathing. 'This is not the time for a panic attack' I think to myself. The only one who notices of course had to be Dante. He immediately runs over to me and gets on the ground.

"Out" he tells Antonio and Aphrodite in a calm voice. They listen but don't shut the door this time. "Athena, look at me please" he says, staying calm. I look at him still not being able to breath well.

"It's ok. I promise" he says standing up. He picks me up and takes me to his room. By the time we get to his room my breathing is better. "W-why are we in here. I thought I wasn't allowed in your room" I say as he sets me down on his bed.

He lays down on the bed and pulls me into his chest. "I wanna make sure your ok. Your sleeping with me" he tells me. I don't have the energy to fight with him so I just go to sleep.

In the morning

I wake up to someone poking my face. I slowly open my eyes and see Luna standing in front of me. "Athena... Anastasia is here.." she tells me and I immediately get out of bed.

"Come with me Luna. I need to get dressed" I whisper to Luna, not wanting to wake up Dante. We get to my room and I change as fast as I can.

(Athena's outfit)

(Athena's shoes)

"Where's Anastasia?" I ask Luna as we walk out of my room. "She's downstairs in the living room" she says quietly as we get to the bottom of the stairs.

I immediately walk into the living room. I see Anastasia sitting on the couch wearing another horrible dress.

(Anastasia's dress)

"What are you doing here?" I ask in a fake nice voice. She turns to look at me when she hears my voice. "Me and Dante have a date" she tells me smirking. "If you have a date... why is he still in bed" I ask smiling.

After 5 minutes of them fighting

"Why are you being so bitchy!" Anastasia yells at me. "I'm not" I say shrugging. Before Anastasia can say anything else, Dante walks up behind me. "What's all the yelling?" He asks, not looking at Anastasia, but looking at me instead.

"Anastasia is mad at me. I literally didn't do anything this time" I tell him. I wasn't even lying. "So now that your awake, you guys can go on your date" I say and start walking to the kitchen.

I only take 4 steps before getting pulled back. "What do you mean? I don't have a date with anyone" he says confused. "Anastasia said you guys had a date" I tell him shrugging.

He turns to look at her. "We don't have a date. We've never gone on a date" he says. "Exactly! Other couples go on dates but we don't!" Anastasia yells at Dante.

"We aren't a couple! We have never been a couple!" Dante yells back louder. "Dante, be nice, she's delusional remember" I say smirking at her. "I've noticed" he says laughing.

"Get out of my house" Dante tells Anastasia, and she immediately runs out. "I'm taking a day off work so I'll watch Luna today" Dante tells me.

6 hours later

I have been drawing for hours so I decided to take a break and shower. I get up, grab a towel and go to my bathroom.

Dante's POV

I walk into Athena's room. I needed to talk to her about last night. I hear the shower so I decide to wait for her. I walk over to her bed and sit down.

I see her sketch book laying open on her bed and decide to look through it. There's only 2 drawings in the book.

Chapter 7

Back to Athena's pov

I walk up to him and snatch my sketchbook out of his hands. "Don't touch my shit!" I yell annoyed. He looks at me, angry.

"Don't fucking yell at me! It's literally just drawings!" He yells back. "That doesn't matter! You wouldn't like it if I went through your stuff so don't go through mine!" I yell back.

He suddenly stands up and walks up to me. "Do not disrespect me. You are in my house, I can do what I want" he says sounding annoyed. "So I get no privacy?" I ask also annoyed.

"It's a fucking sketchbook. Get over it" he says, walking out of my room. "Fucking asshole" I mumble, getting into bed.

The next morning

"Athena... wake up" I hear a familiar voice whisper in my ear. I slowly open my eyes, Luna's face becoming clear. "Is something wrong Luna?" I ask a bit concerned.

"Nope! I just wanted you to get up!" She says, raising her voice. "Seriously Luna" I groan, getting out of bed. "What time is it?" I ask her while changing.

"9" she tells me shrugging. "Oh shit" I yell as a cut my hand on the knife in my drawer. Dante immediately runs into my room concerned. "What happened?! Why did you yell?!" He says fast, running over to me.

"I'm fine, just cut myself.." I tell him, trying to calm him down. "On what?! I took your kn-" he starts to say but stops himself. "Luna, why don't you go to your room so I can talk to Athena" Dante tells Luna and Luna walks out.

"Do you mind doing me a favour?" Dante asks while following me into my bathroom. "Depends on what it is" I tell him, cleaning up the cut on my hand.

"There's a ball tonight and I need a date, but I don't wanna go with a stranger. So I was wondering if you would go with me... and pretend to be my girlfriend?" He says quietly but still loud enough for me to hear him.

"Sure. Theme?" I ask. I've always wanted to go to a ball. "I have a dress for you, but do you know how to do makeup?" He asks, surprised I said yes.

"Yup, just give me the dress and I'll match my makeup to the dress" I tell him and he nods, walking out to get the dress while I finish cleaning my cut.

After about 10 minutes Dante walks in with a black dress in his hands. "Try it on to make sure it fits" he tells me while handing me the dress. I take the dress and go put it on in my bathroom.

(Athena's dress)

I walk out of my bathroom with the dress on. "It fits perfectly" I say, startling him a bit because he wasn't paying attention. "Holy shit.." he says smirking.

"We have like 5 hours till we have to go. So you can do whatever till then, just make sure your ready by 5" he tells me and walks out of my room.

I decide there's no point in taking the dress off and go back into my bathroom to do my makeup.

The makeup takes 2 hours

(The makeup look)

Once I finish my makeup I sit on my bed and think about what else I need. Suddenly Aphrodite bursts into my room with something in her hand.

"Bitch you didn't tell me you were going to the ball! Also I have earring for you!!" She yells and starts putting the earrings in my ears.

(The earrings)

"Ok there! Also necklace! Get up and turn around" she says and I do what she told me to. She puts the necklace on me.

(The necklace)"Perfect!!!" Aphrodite yells. "You look fucking amazing by the wayyy!!" She says while walking out of my room. I hope this ball goes well.

_____Thank you all for being so patient with me!

Sorry for the short chapter again and sorry for the little cliffhanger again.

I'm trying to write more but my mental health isn't the best still.

I love you all and thanks for reading!!

Chapter 8

"Athena, are you ready?" Dante asks walking into my room. "Yup" I say getting off my bed. I walk up to Dante and he hands me gloves. "Put these on" he says.

(The gloves)

I put them on and we walk downstairs. "Well hello there beautiful" I hear a familiar voice say. I look around to see Mark smiling at me. "Mark!" I yell, happy to see a familiar face.

"Come on. We are gonna be late" Dante says grabbing my hand. We walk outside and get in the car.

When they get to the ball

Dante gets out first and runs around the car. He opens my door and helps me out of the car. "Such a gentleman" I say giggling quietly. He looks at me with a fake offended face.

"I'm always a gentleman" he says, closing the car door. "Sure you are" I say as we start walking towards the building. When we walk in a guy immediately walks up to us.

"Hello Dante! Oh, who might this be?" The person says. "None of your business, Marco" Dante responds. "Oh come on dear brother, scared I'm gonna steal your little slut?" Marco says, informing me that they are brothers.

"She's not a slut, she's my girlfriend. Plus you don't have a chance with her. She's out of your league" Dante says with a straight face. "Vattene prima che ti spari" Dante says, but I don't understand.(Translation- Walk away before I shoot you)

"Whatever, she's not even that pretty anyway" Marco says, walking away.

"Don't listen to him. He's just jealous" Dante tells me, turning to face me. We start walking to the bar but get stopped by a familiar guy.

"Athena, what are you doing here?!" I recognise the voice immediately.

I get closer to Dante. "Hi Eris... I'm Dante's-" I start saying but I get cut off. "She's my girlfriend. Who are you?" Dante says, sounding a bit angry and confused.

"Woah, he's a bit overprotective isn't he?" Eris says laughing. When he notices we aren't laughing he stops. "I'm her ex" he tells Dante looks at me then looks back at Eris.

"Well, good to know I never had any competition" Dante says, smirking. Eris looks at Dante with an annoyed look. "You wanna fucking fight?!" Eris asks, obviously angry.

"Sure. My place, tomorrow, 11am, don't be late" Dante says and gives Eris the address. "I'll be there" Eris says, walking away. Once he's gone I turn to Dante.

"What the fuck was that?!" I say trying to keep my voice down. "He was eye-fucking you. I couldn't just let him eye-fuck my girlfriend" he says.

"I'm not actually your girlfriend and you know that! Plus I can deal with my own problems!" I whisper. "So you admit he was a problem to you" Dante says smiling because he knows he won.

"Just don't kill him tomorrow, please" I say as I walk to the bar. "No promises" he says following behind me. I roll my eyes but don't say anything back.

"Hello beautiful, what can I get you?" the bartender asks me. Suddenly, I feel hot breathe on my neck. I immediately know it's Dante. "Whiskey. For both of us" Dante says.

The bartender looks at me to see if that's what I want so I nod. When the bartender walks away to get our drinks I tilt my head back to look at Dante.

"I can order my own fucking drink! I told you this last time!" I say really angry. "I know you can, but he called my girlfriend beautiful and I didn't like it" he says with no emotion on his face.

"Stop being so jealous and protective! I'm not actually your girl-friend!" I whisper, getting really angry. He ignores what I said.

"Tu me traites comme un putain d'enfant et j'en ai marre!" I mumble to myself.(Translation- You treat me like a fucking child and I'm fucking sick of it!)

Dante walks around talking to people with Athena by his side the whole time

_____Thank you for reading!!!

Sorry for the short chapter again!!

I love you all and thank you so much for waiting!

I know I don't publish chapters that much but I really try. I haven't had a lot of time lately but I will try my best to publish more chapters!!

Have a good day/night everyone!!!

Chapter 9

They go home and go to bed immediately

In the morning

"Athena, wake up" I hear Dante whispering "Mmmm go away" I say turning away. "Athena you need to get up" Dante tells me in a normal voice.

"No I don't. Luna is with your parents for 2 weeks so I get to sleep in" I tell him as if he didn't know where his own Daughter was. "Did you forget I'm fighting Eris today?" He says and I immediately sit up.

I jump out of bed and run into my closet. "Shit shit shit" I mumble to myself. I grab a dress and a pair of heels. I bring my outfit into the bathroom and get changed.

(The dress)

I put on the dress and bring the heels over to my bed. I sit on the bed and put the heels on.

(The heels)

"Done!" I say out of breath. "Well that's good cause we have 10 minutes till he gets here" Dante tells me and we go to the basement. In the basement is the training area.

"Be careful, and please let me do the-" Dante starts to say but gets cut off by Eris. "I'm here bitch" Eris says walking in like he's the king. I just roll my eyes.

"I see you still dress like your 5 Athena" Eris says laughing. "I see you still act like your 5 Eris" I spit back. "That's not very nice Athena" Eris says, not laughing anymore but still smiling.

"Can we just get this fight over with" Dante says, getting impatient. "Of course bitch boy" Eris responds. "Athena!" Aphrodite yells running up to me.

"Let's go bitch we are gonna go get matching tattoos!" Aphrodite yells again and grabs my hand, dragging me back upstairs. "Thank you for taking me out of that situation! I really didn't want to watch them fight" I thank Aphrodite.

"No problem bestie! But we are going to get matching tattoos" she tells me and we go out to her car. We get in and she drives to the tattoo place.

At the tattoo place

"Yo bitch!" Aphrodite yells at the tattoo artist. "2 tattoos. Matching. Me and this bitch beside me. Now!" She yells again. This surprises me.

The tattoo artist immediately gets another person to tattoo me while he tattoos Aphrodite.

(Their matching tattoos)

Once the tattoos were done they went home

"We're home!!!" Me and Aphrodite yell while laughing. The house is silent. Completely silent. "Maybe they are in the basement" Aphrodite suggests and we walk downstairs. I immediately see Eris laying on the ground.

Blood all over his face. "What the fuck Dante!" Aphrodite yells. I couldn't say anything. I was frozen in shock. "Athena!" I hear Dante yell but I couldn't respond.

Dante ran up to me and reached out for me. I immediately moved away. "Don't put your hands on me! I told you not to fucking kill him!" I yell angry and scared at the same time.

"I didn't fucking kill him! He's still breathing you bitch!!" Dante yells back. I stare at him with hurt in my eyes. His face changes to regret. "Fuck you Dante. Don't speak to me again" I say with a voice.

I run out and go to my room. I didn't know what to do. I went into my closet and started packing a bag. I couldn't live with him anymore. I was half way done packing when I realised...

_____New chapter everyone!!!!

Another short chapter I'm so so sorry!

Im trying to write more I promise! Sorry for taking to long to finish this chapter!!

I love you all and thank you so much for reading!!

Chapter 10

I couldn't leave Luna. I love her like she's my own. She looks up to me. I can't leave her, I won't leave her. Suddenly Aphrodite runs into my closet.

She sits on the floor with me and pulls me into a hug. "Are you ok?" She asks, concerned. "I don't know. I want to quit so I don't have to see him anymore but I don't want to leave Luna" I tell her.

"I think you should stay just make sure you only talk to him about Luna from now on" she tells me, getting up. She holds her hand out for me and I take it. She helps me up and gives me another hug.

"Tomorrow we are going out and getting our nails done together, ok?" She says. I nod and she smiles. She walks out of my room and I go put on my pj's.

(You can pick her pj's- please leave the link in the comments cause I'm interested to see what y'all pick)

I go sit in my bed and grab my book off my nightstand.

After reading for an hour

My head shoots up as someone barges into my room. It was Dante. "I'm sorry for calling you a bitch" he says and I cover my head with my blanket.

He walks over to my bed and sits by my feet. "Please talk to me" he says sounding guilty. "Just go away" I say quietly. "Athena, I didn't mean what I said. You don't understand" He says.

I uncover myself and sit up. "What don't I understand?! Come on explain it to me! I would really like to know what you think I don't understand, because I'm pretty sure I understand completely!" I yell, angry.

He just stares down at his lap. "Come on! Fucking speak! If your going to sit here and tell me I don't understand then you need to fucking explain it to me!" I yell getting impatient.

"Eris said something that made me angry and I took some of my anger out on you!" He yells back. "Don't fucking yell at me! You don't get the right to yell at me! How the fuck did you have any anger left after almost KILLING Eris!!" I yell back.

"He said you are a fucking whore that dresses like a child. Told me I should fire you because your gonna seduce me and then leave. I told him you would never do that no matter what. Even if I made you mad you would never leave Luna. Told him you've only known Luna for a month and she already sees you as her mom" he tells me calmly.

After sitting in silence for 10 minutes

"I'm sorry" I say. He nods and walks out. I just go to sleep.

In the morning

"Wake up Athena, we are going to get our nails done" I hear Aphrodite say and I sit up in bed. "Ok ok ok, just let me get dressed" I say and walk into my closet.

_____Im so sorry for not publishing any chapters lately I haven't had time with school!!

A really short chapter sorryyy!

I really love you all and thank you so much for staying with me!

Chapter 11

"Hurry up and get dressed!" Aphrodite yells at me sitting in my bed as I walk into my closet.

(Athena's dress)

(Athena's shoes)

(Aphrodite's dress)

(Aphrodite's shoes)

I walk out of my closet dressed. "Alright I'm ready I just have to go tell Dante that I'm leaving" I tell Aphrodite. We both leave my room and I walk down the hall to Dante's office.

Instead of knocking I just walk in. I immediately see Anastasia naked on his desk. I scream and cover my eyes, turning and walking out. I close the door and run downstairs where Aphrodite is sitting on the couch waiting for me.

I lay down on the couch and cover my face with a pillow. "Athena what the fuck happened?" Aphrodite asks while taking the pillow away from me.

"I just saw that whore NAKED!" I yell feeling traumatized. "What?!" She says sounding angry. Suddenly Dante is running down the stairs and towards us looking angry.

I hide my face in Aphrodites neck, scared. "Athena what the fuck is wrong with you?! Your supposed to knock!" He yells. I take my head out of Aphrodites neck and stare at him with wide eyes.

"That's what your concerned about?! Me not knocking?! Not the fact that I just saw that whore NAKED?!" I yell somewhat angry but mostly sad. "You know what, get the fuck out of my house! You have 2 hours to get your stuff and leave" he says and walks away.

I don't have the energy to do anything so I go up to my room and start packing my stuff. "Athena I'm not letting you leave" Aphrodite says walking into my room.

"I don't have a choice. He kicked me out Aphrodite I'm sorry" I say, tears rolling down my face. She walks out angry.

1 and a half hours later and Athena is done packing

Dante walks in my room, his face full of regret. "Athena your not leaving. I didn't mean to say that" he says coming and sitting on the floor with me.

"You can't take back what you said" I tell him moving away from him. "Athena please you can't leave me" he whispers curling up into a ball. Anastasia walks in without even knocking.

"Baby come on. She'll be out in 25 minutes and then we can go back to what we didn't get to finish" she says trying to seduce him. "Anastasia if you don't get the fuck out I will kill you!" He yells.

She looks at him shocked then looks at me. "What did you say to him you little bitch!" She yells at me walking over to me and grabs me. "Get your hands off of me whore!" I yell trying to push her off.

"I'll kill you! You ruined everything!" She yells not letting go of me. I grab my knife off my bed and stab her leg. She finally lets go screaming and holds her leg. "YOU BITCH" she yells and I run into my bathroom and lock the door.

I put my back on the door and slowly slide to the floor crying.

20 minutes later

"Athena please come out she's not even in the house anymore" Dante says trying to get me to leave the bathroom. "No" I say still crying. "You can't just stay in there forever" He tells me.

"Yes I can. I have food and water in here. That's all I need" I tell him still not wanting to let anyone in. "Come on please let me in" he says. No response.

"Athena? Athena please respond! I know your mad at me but you can't just ignore me!" He says getting anxious. "Athena if you don't respond right now I'm gonna break the door down!" He yells, banging on the door.

No response.

_____Sorry for the short chapter again I just haven't had any motivation lately!

Cliffhanger!! Guess in the comments why you think Athena wasn't responding!!

Chapter 12

Dante's POV

"Aphrodite! Help!" I yell. Athena is laying on the ground not responding to me. Aphrodite comes running in. She sees Athena and just sits beside her.

She picks Athena's head up and sets it on her lap. "Why aren't you freaking out!" I yell, scared. "She has low iron. This has happened so many times I promise she will be fine just give her a few minutes. In the meantime go get me a glass of water" she tells me in a calm tone.

20 minutes later Athena is conscious

"I'm so sorry Athena! I promise Anastasia and me didn't do anything together" I tell her. She's laying in her bed now but refuses to talk to me. Anastasia and me really didn't do anything.

"Athena please don't ignore me. I didn't do anything with her! I love you Not her!" I say starting to cry. I've never cried in front of anyone before, but I feel so comfortable with Athena. I know I can trust her.

I leave her alone assuming she's annoyed with me at this point

The next day

Athena's POV

"Is this really a good idea?" I ask Aphrodite. She convinced me to dye my hair today. "Yes! You will look so good once it's done!" She says really excited. She's always wanted to dye my hair for some reason.

Once her hair is dyed

(Athena's hair now)

"Now that we are done with that. How would you feel about going down to the training room with me? We could throw knives or shoot, anything you want to do" Aphrodite says knowing I don't like going down there.

"As long as you don't leave me down there alone then yes" I tell her. She hates going down alone and so do I. Luna is at her grandparents house for the week so I have nothing to do.

"Can I choose our outfits! Pleaseeeeeee!" She says. "Not this time" I say annoyed and go grab the outfit I left in my room.

(Aphrodite's outfit and shoes)

(Athena's outfit and shoes)

"Here take this" Aphrodite says throwing me a gun.

(The gun)(They have matching ones the blue is Athena's and the black is Aphrodites)

"Got you a personalized gun, babe" she says winking at me. I laugh as we walk out of her room and go downstairs. We stop in the kitchen to get water. "Where are you guys going" we hear behind us as we are filling our bottles.

I turn to look at him. "We are going down to the training room. We were just filling our bottles" I tell him. "Why are you going down there?" He asks, his question obviously targeting me.

"Because we want to" Aphrodite tells him, taking my hand. We walk out of the kitchen and go down to the basement where the training room is.

Immediately, all the guys in the room turn towards us, just staring. I decide to ignore the stares and just walk up to the shooting area. "This isn't a place for little girls, honey" a random guy says to me.

I hear the door open to the training room but don't look. "I'm not a little girl. I'm 22" I tell him while loading my gun. "Does Dante know your down here?" He asks.

"Yes he does" I say trying to end the conversation until he tries to take my gun out of my hands. "Hey! What the fuck!" I say when he gets it out of my hands. "That's my fucking gun you dick!" I yell.

"Your to little to have a gun" he tells me laughing. "Give her the gun back" I hear from behind me. "Dante, it's a real gun. Little girls can't handle guns" the guy says with a surprised look on his face.

"I said give Athena her fucking gun!" Dante yells, making me flint really bad. They both look at me confused and the guy gives me my gun. I take it from him and look back at the targets.

I shoot 5 times, hitting the middle of the target every time. Both guys look at me as if I fucking killed someone. "Where did you learn to do that?" Dante asks me with obvious surprise in his voice.

"I taught myself when my parents abandoned me. I needed to be able to defend myself" I say shrugging. "What other skills do you have?" Dante asks me. "I can throw knives pretty well" I tell him.

He brings me over to another area and hands me 5 knifes. I look at what I'm throwing at and see fake body's. "I'm gonna tell you what to hit" he tells me as I get into position. "Right shoulder" he says and I immediately throw a knife hitting the right shoulder.

"Left knee" he says and I immediately throw another knife hitting the left knee. "Right ankle" he says and I wait a second before throwing the knife, I hit the right ankle.

"Heart" he says and I throw the knife right into the heart. "This one is gonna be a bit more difficult" he tells me and I just nod. "Between the eyes" he says and a second later theres a knife between the eyes of the fake body.

"Come to my office" he says and without another word he's dragging me to his office. Once we get to his office I sit down and wait for him to speak. "Why didn't you tell me you had the skills to be in the mafia?" He asks confused.

"Because I don't" I don't feel like telling him the real reason. "You do though. There's tryout tomorrow, would you please just come tryout tomorrow?" He asks practically begging me.

"Maybe another time. I don't want a different job right now" I don't wanna stop taking care of Luna. "Ok. You can go now" he tells me sounding disappointed.

"I'm sorry" I say walking out of his office.

_____Longer than usual!! Hope y'all like this chapter and sorry for not publishing any recently!!

Love you all!!

Chapter 13

I go back to the training room looking around for Aphrodite. I finally find her and start walking towards her. "Je jure devant Dieu que tu es tellement stupide" I hear her say in French and I giggle.(Translation- I swear to god you are so stupid)

The guy she's talking to looks at me, giving me the death stare. I stand beside Aphrodite and look at her. "ce qui se passe" I ask confused. (Translation- What is happening)

"You stupid french whore! Get out! Your not allowed to be here! You fucking spy!" The guy starts yelling at me and pulls out his gun. I put my hands up, laughing a bit.

"What the fuck are you laughing about?!" He yells, still pointing his gun at me. I hear Antonio and Dante walking up to us confused on why this guy is yelling.

The guy looks at them with a smile. "Boss! Come over here!" He says "This stupid French whore is a French spy! She came over here for no reason and started talking to Aphrodite in French!" He explains to Dante and Antonio, with a smirk on his face.

Dante and Antonio stare at me for a good 10 seconds and then start laughing. "Oh my god he called her a stupid French whore" Antonio says, still laughing. "se non smetti di ridere penso che ti ucciderà" Aphrodite says pointing at me. (Translation- if you do not stop laughing I think she is going to kill you)

They stop laughing when they see me glaring at them. "Can you help me out! He's pointing a fucking gun at me!!" I yell at them, annoyed. They turn to the guy and look at the gun he has pointed at me.

Dante takes the gun from him and looks at him, angry. "fottuto idiota, non è una spia francese, è la mia fottuta ragazza! scusati subito prima che ti spari in testa" Dante says to the guy, in an angry tone. (Translation- you fucking idiot she is not a french spy she is my fucking girlfriend! apologise right now before I shoot you in the head)

The guy, Aphrodite and Antonio all look surprised at what he said but I was just standing there confused. "I'm so sorry ma'am I didn't know you were his" the guy says with fear in his voice.

"ora scusati per averla chiamata stupida puttana" Dante says, a bit calmer. "I'm so sorry for calling you a stupid whore ma'am. It will never happen again" the guy says to me, fear still obvious in his voice.(Translation- now apologise for calling her a stupid whore)

The guy walks away and I immediately turn to Dante. "What did you say to him?" I ask, a bit concerned. "None of your concern Athena" he says, no emotion in his voice now. He starts walking away and I follow him.

"Dante tell me what you said!" I yell getting annoyed with him. "I already told you it's none of your concern" he says continuing to walk away. I follow him all the way to his office and walk in with him, slamming the door behind me.

When I turn back to look at him he's already sitting at his desk with a surprised look on his face. "So tell me why he said he didn't know I was yours. You will also tell me why the guy, Aphrodite, and Antonio all looked at you surprise after you said whatever the fuck you said!" I demand, standing in front of his desk.

He suddenly stands up making me flinch a bit. "You do not have the fucking right to demand anything from me! I am your boss and you will listen to me! You are a nobody!" He yells at me.

I look at him, obviously hurt by his words. "Ok" I say, a sad tone in my voice. I start walking to the door but he gets up and blocks the door. "Please move Dante. This conversation is over. You made yourself clear" I say, just wanting to leave.

"Fuck, I'm sorry for calling you a nobody. I didn't mean a word I said. Please just sit down and I'll tell you what I said to that fucking dumbass" he says, guilt all over his face.

I think about it and decide to listen to what he has to say. I stand in front of his desk and he sits down behind it. "You want what I said word for word or do you just want what I said over all" he asks, looking down.

"Word for word" I say. "The first thing I said was, you fucking idiot she is not a french spy she is my fucking girlfriend. Apologise right now before I shoot you in the head" he tells me, still looking down. "What was the second thing you said" I ask, still processing what he just told me.

"Now apologise for calling her a stupid whore" he says, finally looking up at me. I stare at him in shock, not knowing how to respond. "You told him I'm your girlfriend" I mumble walking over to the couch in his office and sitting down.

"I'm sorry. It just came out. I didn't think before I said it" he rambles. "You told him I'm your girlfriend" I mumble again, still in shock.

"That's why Aphrodite and Antonio looked so surprised" I said, moving to lay down on the couch.

_____New chapter everyone!!!

I hope everyone likes it!!

There's a lot of Italian and French in this chapter so please tell me if something is wrong as I do not know Italian nor French, I'm just using Google translate and I know it can be wrong

I love you all and appreciate everyone that has stuck with me so far!!

You guys have gotten this book so high in ranks!

#6 in fighting#112 in protective#47 in French#42 in swearing#23 in knives#29 in darkromance

I really do appreciate all the support and hope I can get some more chapters out before I have to go back to school for exams

Love you all and hope you had an amazing holiday!!

Chapter 14

"Athena, are you ok..?" Dante asks me, walking over to me. I don't respond to him, instead I just stare at the ceiling.

20 minutes later

"Sono troppo occupato per affrontare i tuoi stupidi errori in questo momento!" I hear Dante yelling at someone on the phone in Italian. Still laying on the couch, I wondered who he was talking to and what he was saying.(Translation- I'm too busy to deal with your stupid mistakes right now)

Dante hangs up and groans. "Is everything ok?" I ask him. It's the only thing I've said in 20 minutes. "Yup everything's perfect" he says sarcastically and I frown.

"Tu penses que je suis stupide. Me mentir comme si je ne connaissais pas la vérité" I say, knowing he doesn't understand French. "What did you just say Athena" he asks, annoyed.(Translation- You think I'm stupid. Lying to me like I don't know the truth)

"Nothing" I mumble, loud enough so he can hear me. "Athena, tell me what you fucking said!" He yells. He slams his hand down on his desk, making a really loud sound. I flinch at the sound.

"I said your stupid!" I yell annoyed that he yelled at me. He stands up fast and walks over to me. "Excuse me" he says, really angry. "Sorry, I forgot you are deaf, let me say it louder for you. YOUR STUPID!!" I scream sitting up.

"Get. Out." He says, but I don't move. "Athena, get the fuck out!" He yells at me, making me flinch again. I get up and run out of his office. I go to my room and slam the door behind me.

I get changed into my pyjamas and start crying.

(Athena's pyjamas)

1 hour later

I'm still crying a bit when someone knocks on my door. I don't respond. A few seconds later I hear Dante. "Athena I know your in there. Can I please come in?" He asks calmly.

"I guess" I say, sniffling. He comes into my room, closing the door behind him. He sits down on my bed, not looking at me. "I'm sorry for yelling at you and for slamming my hand on my desk... I know it scared you.." he says.

"It didn't scare me.." I tell him, obviously lying. "Athena, I saw you flinch" he tells me making me sigh. "That doesn't mean anything" I say, sitting up in my bed. "Athena, please stop lying to me. I'm not that stupid" he says, making me laugh.

"What are you laughing about?" He asks finally looking at me, and finally smiling. "You said your NoT tHaT StUPid" I say mocking his voice, still laughing. He looks at me confused.

"You just admitted your stupid" I explain while laughing. He looks at me like I'm insane. Once I stop I stare at him while smiling. "What are you smiling for?" He asks me, also smiling.

"You look so cute when you smile" I tell him. "I'm not cute" he says, frowning. "Yes you are" I say getting up and walk into my bathroom, leaving the door open. "I am not" he groans walking to my bathroom, standing in the doorway.

I grab my toothbrush and get it ready. "You can deny it all you want but we both know you are so very cute" I tell me. I start brushing my teeth and he walks into my bathroom, standing behind me. "I'm not cute, I'm hot" he states, wrapping his arms around my waist.

He stares at me, in the mirror, over my shoulder. I finish brushing my teeth and just stand there. "Dante.. is something wrong?" I ask him, confused. I turn to face him. "Everything's fine" he says while looking down at me, keeping his arms around my waist.

"Can you please let me go?" I ask, looking up at him. "No I don't really want to" he says, like he's a child. I laugh at him. "Dante you have to go deal with whatever that call was about" I tell him. "No I told them that I'm busy" he tells me, smiling.

"And what are you busy with?" I ask. "You" he tells me, making me blush. "Your putting off work for me?" I ask surprised. "I will always put you before work" he says, picking me up. "Dante, you never put off work for anyone what's going on?" I ask.

"Nothings going on, I promise. Now what do you want to do" he asks me, carrying me out of my room. "Will you come train with me? I don't wanna go without you" I explain. Instead of responding he carries me down to the training room.

He puts me down and wraps his arms around my waist again. "What do-" Dante starts to talk but gets cut off by a random group of men. "She's hot" one of them says. "Yeah she is. Can I have her after your done with her Dante" another one says.

"I call her after you" someone yells. 3 guys start arguing about who gets me. "All of you shut the fuck up!" Dante yells making them all stop talking. "All 3 of you, my office, NOW" he says and they all run out of the training room.

"Your coming with me. I don't want to leave you down here alone" Dante tells me and I nod. Dante holds my hand and we walk to his office. When we get to his office I see all 3 guys sitting in front of Dante's desk.

Dante doesn't let go of my hand, instead he brings me behind his desk and sits down. He pulls me onto his lap. "Luca, Matteo, Lorenzo, You will say sorry to la mia ragazza and explain why you thought what you all said was ok!" He says, raising his voice. The anger in his voice makes me flinch a bit.(Translation- my girlfriend)

Dante notices this and rubs my thigh. "I am very sorry ma'am" Luca says. "I apologize for what I said ma'am" Lorenzo says. "Well I'm not sorry for what I said bitch" Matteo says, surprising all of us.

"Je ne suis pas la garce ici" I mumble. "She's French?! Your dating a fucking French bitch?!" Matteo yells, getting up. "Matteo! Sit the fuck down before I shoot you!" Dante yells and I turn to look at him. "Stop yelling, it hurts my head" I tell him. (Translation- I'm not the bitch here)

"I'm sorry" Dante says, guilt in his voice. "Lorenzo, Luca, you can both go. Matteo sit the fuck down" he says. Matteo groans and sits down while Luca and Lorenzo leave. "Matteo, I have already gone through this today. Just because she speaks French doesn't mean she's a spy. Apologize to her now" Dante says as calm as he possibly can.

"I'm sorry for saying I want you after Dante is done with you and for calling you a bitch" Matteo groans. "Leave" Dante says and Matteo walks out of his office. "Athena what's wrong?" He asks me.

"I'm tired" I tell him. He puts one arm under my legs, his other arm on my upper back and stands up. He carries me to his room and puts me down on his bed. He goes into his bathroom and comes out in black sweatpants and no shirt.

He lays down beside me. "Why am I in here?" I ask him. "Because I want you to be in here" he tells me. I turn away from him and close my eyes. I feel one of his arms on my waist, he moves me so my back is pressed up against his chest.

We both fall asleep in that position.

Chapter 15

I wake up and try to get out of bed, but I get pulled back. "Stay" I hear Dante mumble. "Dante, I want to go train I didn't really get to yesterday" I tell him and he lets me get out of bed.

"I'm coming with you. Go change and meet me in the kitchen" he tells me, I nod and go to my room to get dressed. I don't plan on doing anything other than target practice so I put on a dress.

(Athena's dress)

I quickly put on boots and run down to the kitchen.

(Athena's boots)

I see Dante filling up 2 water bottles. I sneak up behind him. "Boo!" I yell, making him jump a bit. "Athena don't do that! You scared me!"

He raises his voice, hugging me. "I'm sorry" I say and grab one of the bottles. "You didn't even change you just put on a shirt" I tell him.

"So?" He says as we start walking to the training room. "You told me that I had to change" I say as we arrive outside the training room. He pulls me into him quickly and looks down at me. "I told you to change because we are going into a room full of men and what you were wearing showed to much" he whispers.

"Oh.. I'm sorry I didn't know" I say, blushing. "Don't say sorry. I liked it, but I don't want my men seeing you in that" he says, making me blush more. I nod and we go into the training room.

I immediately walk towards the side room that has all the guns in it but someone stands in front of me. "Can you move?" I ask, trying to be nice. "Little girls don't belong in here sweetheart" the guy says looking down at me. "What's the issue now" Dante groans behind me.

I turn around to face him. "This guy just said LiTle GirLs DOn't BeLoNg iN HeRE SwEeTHeaRt and he refuses to move" I tell Dante mocking the guys voice when I tell Dante what he said. "Are you mocking me little girl?!" The guy raises his voice.

"Yes I am. Do you have a problem?" I say turning back to the guy.

"Yeah I do have a problem! Don't fucking mock me!" He says, looking very angry. "Awww but you can't do anything about it" I say in a condescending tone. He pulls out a gun and points it at me.

"Oh no I'm so scared!" I say, still in a condescending tone. I pull out a gun that I had strapped to my thigh. "You think I'm stupid?" I say, pointing the gun between his eyes. "Put your gun on the floor or your fucking dead" I say. He slowly puts his gun on the floor and puts his hands up.

"Dante, please take her gun before she kills me" the guy says, fear in his voice. "I don't think I will, Alessandro. You decided to treat her like she's a child so she decided to prove that she isn't" Dante says, wrapping his arms around my waist.

Alessandro looked at Dante's arms with a shocked look on his face. "So she's a whore" Alessandro says. I move the gun and shoot his leg. "I am not a fucking whore!" I yell as Alessandro falls to the floor.

"Dante are you seriously not going to do anything" Alessandro yells. "Actually I am" Dante says. Dante calls over some of his men and talks to them. A minute later Alessandro is being taken away.

"Where are you taking him" I ask Dante. "It doesn't matter. All that matter is he will never be able to insult you again" he tells me. I nod and walk into the room with all the guns.

I grab a random one and walk over to the targets.

1 hour later

I finish training and go look for Dante. I find him with Anastasia. I start walking up to them till I see Anastasia kiss him. I start walking faster and push her away from him.

"Qu'est-ce que tu penses faire, bordel?! Embrasser mon putain d'homme devant moi?!" I yell and hear Aphrodite gasp behind me. (Translation: What the fuck do you think your doing?! Kissing my man in front of me?!)

"Tu viens de l'appeler ton homme?! Êtes-vous enfin en couple?!" Aphrodite says in French, shocked. "je te le dirai plus tard" I say. I pull out my gun again and point it at Anastasia. (First translation: Did you just call him your man?! Are you finally dating?!)(Second translation: I'll tell you later)

"I am not in the fucking mood today bitch!" I yell at her, fear in her eyes. "Dante... control your whore please" she says and I shoot her in the arm making her scream in pain. "I am not the fucking whore here honey" I say and Dante takes my gun from me.

"That's enough shooting people for today Athena" he says, making me frown. "I only shot 2 people today though" I say. "Dante! Can you help me!? She just shot me!" Anastasia yells. Dante hands my gun to Aphrodite and wraps his arms around my waist.

"Why should I help the bitch that called la mia ragazza a whore?" He asks, kissing the top of my head. "Because you love me! Your just pretending to love that whore so Aphrodite doesn't kill you!" She yells at him, confusing me.(Translation: my girlfriend)

"What do you mean?" I ask her making her smirk. "Dante is only being nice to you because he is scared of Aphrodite. He knows that Aphrodite would kill him if he hurt you" she says thinking she won.

"That's not even close to true honey. He's the fucking leader of the Italian mafia and I've seen him yell at Aphrodite with no hesitation. He isn't scared of anyone" I say. "Actually I am scared of 1 person.." he says, embarrassed. "I might be just a little bit scared of you.." he says hiding his face in my neck, making me laugh.

"I'm harmless. Wait no I take that back I just realised I shot 2 people today" I say. "Can someone fucking help me before I die?!" Anastasia yells. "God shut the fuck up your not gonna die" Dante says, taking his face out of my neck.

"Antonio, please take Anastasia out of my house" Dante says, picking me up. "Why do I have to do it" Antonio groans. Dante doesn't respond and just carries me to his office.

---

www.ingramcontent.com/pod-product-compliance
Lightning Source LLC
Chambersburg PA
CBHW082157060225
21587CB00009B/341